W9-DAB-522

GOSCINNY AND UDERZO

PRESENT

An Asterix Adventure

ASTERIX
AND THE
CHARIOT RACE

Written by JEAN-YVES FERRI
Illustrated by DIDIER CONRAD
Translated by ADRIANA HUNTER

Colour by THIERRY MÉBARKI

Orion

ITALY ...

WHAT BETTER SYMBOL OF ITS DAZZLING CIVILISATION THAN ITS WONDERFUL ROADS. THEY ARRIVE, STRAIGHT AND RELIABLE, FROM EVERY CORNER OF THE KNOWN WORLD, AND THEY ALL LEAD TO ROME ...

LVPVS GARVM
THE ORIGINAL

ROMA →
← ROMA
VII

CLANG

WHAT CAN I SAY! ALL IN SUCH A HURRY TO GET TO ROME, RUSH, RUSH, RUSH AND THEY DON'T SEE THE POTHOLES!

NERVUS BREAKDOWN
RECOVERY

IN ROME, SOME TIME LATER ...

POTHOLES, PRECISELY! WHICH IS WHY

I HAVE A DREAM!

I HAVE A DREAM THAT PUBLIC FUNDS SHALL GO TOWARDS MAINTAINING OUR ROMAN ROADS AND NOT INTO FUNDING SENATOR LACTUS BIFIDUS'S ORGIES.

SPQR

PSSST, BIFIDUS! WAKE UP, THIS IS ABOUT YOU!

THERE'S MOUNTING ANGER IN THE REGIONS ABOUT THE DEPLORABLE STATE OF OUR ROMAN ROADS!

L-LIES! I, LACTUS BIFIDUS, HAVE RESPONSIBILITY FOR ROMAN ROADS, AND I CANNOT ACCEPT THESE ALLEGATIONS!

SO I'D LIKE TO TAKE THIS OPPORTUNITY TO ANNOUNCE A SPECIAL ONE-OFF CHARIOT RACE!

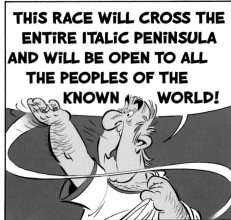

THIS RACE WILL CROSS THE ENTIRE ITALIC PENINSULA AND WILL BE OPEN TO ALL THE PEOPLES OF THE KNOWN WORLD!

IT WILL BE A SPLENDID SHOWCASE FOR THE EXCELLENT STATE OF OUR ROMAN ROADS!

THIS RACE IS A STROKE OF GENIUS! THERMOCUMULUS ALMOST HAD STEAM COMING OUT OF HIS EARS! DID IT COME TO YOU JUST LIKE THAT?

JUST LIKE THAT... I'M FULL OF IDEAS WHEN I FIRST WAKE UP!

THE ONLY PROBLEM IS WE NOW HAVE A RACE TO ORGANISE AND THE ROAD NETWORK'S A NIGHTMARE ...

I KNOW, I'M IN CHARGE OF IT.

* LIBYA

SOME TIME LATER WE FIND OURSELVES IN DARIORITUM* IN ARMORICA WHICH IS HOSTING THE ITINERANT MARKETPLACE FOR ARTEFACTS OF EXCELLENCE (IMAX) ... AND IN THE CROWD WE RECOGNISE A FEW OF OUR FAMILIAR GAULS ...

* VANNES IN BRITTANY

FRESH HONEY BEER

THE HAPPY GOTH
SPECIAL: WILD BOAR SAUERKRAUT

GNSSS

WAH! WAH!

HANG ON IN THERE, GERIATRIX! WE'LL FIND YOU YOUR TOOTH-PULLER!

MY TOOTH! I SHOULDN'T HAVE CRACKED THAT NUT!

SICAN ESES

EGGS & PIGEONS

O HANDSOME GINGER! SHOW YOUR HAND TO THE SIBYL!

OH! I SEE SOMETHING WEIGHING HEAVILY ON YOU, A GREAT BURDEN ...

YES, I'M IN MENHIRS ...

NOT FOR LONG. I SEE A FINE WINGED CHARIOT! PEOPLE ARE CARRYING YOU, CHEERING YOU, YOU'RE BEING CROWNED AS CHAMPION!

A WINGED CHARIOT? ARE YOU SURE?

OBELIX! WHAT ARE YOU DOING? WE'RE WAITING!

HURRY UP! THIS TOOTH IS KILLING GERIATRIX!

GNSSS! I'M TOO YOUNG TO DIE ...

THE SIBYL SAID I'M GOING TO BE A GREAT AURIGA ...*

PFFF! SHE'S TAKING YOU FOR A RIDE.

AH! HERE'S THE STALL.

* A CHARIOTEER

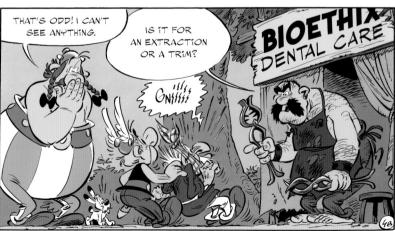

THAT'S ODD! I CAN'T SEE ANYTHING.

IS IT FOR AN EXTRACTION OR A TRIM?

GNSSS

BIOETHIX DENTAL CARE

THE END OF TRADITIONAL MENHIRS!

INSIST ON GENUINE VESUVIAN PUMICE!

WE ALSO HAVE THIS MAGNIFICENT GAULISH WINGED SPORTS CHARIOT!

A LITTLE LATER ...

YOU SEE, GERIATRIX, IT WASN'T ALL THAT BAD!

BY BELENOFF! I FEEL LIKE A FIKFTEEN-YEAR-OLD!

AND PLUFF I'LL GET A NEW ONE. IT WAV A MILK TOOF ... UNLEFF HE WAV LYING THROUGH HIS TEEF.

AH! THERE'S OBELIX.

I FOLLOWED MY INSTINCTS.

?!

WHAT'S THAT CHARIOT FOR, OBELIX?

WHAT? THERE'S MORE TO LIFE THAN MENHIRS ...

WELL DONE, OBELIKF! YOU HAVE TO DO VEVE FINGS WHEN YOU'RE YOUNG!

HOW DID YOU PAY FOR IT?

THE SALESMAN SAID I COULD PAY ON CREDIT. TEN INSTALMENTS OF EIGHT MENHIRS: A BARGAIN!

OBELIX, YOU DO REALISE THAT SORT OF CHARIOT IS MEANT FOR RACING AND ...

GET YOUR "CONDATUM ECHO"!

ALL THE DETAILS OF THE GREAT TRANSITALIC RACE!

THE CONDATUM ECHO

A CHARIOT RACE ON ROMAN SOIL? HEHE! WHY NOT?

IT MIGHT BE FUN BOTHERING THEM ON THEIR HOME TURF FOR ONCE!

YOU CAN'T BECOME AN AURIGA OVERNIGHT, OBELIX! YOU WERE A MENHIR DELIVERYMAN LAST TIME I LOOKED!

PAH! TRADITIONAL MENHIRS ARE HAVING A DOWNTURN BECAUSE OF PUMICE STONE COPIES.

... AND THE SIBYL AT THE MARKETPLACE SAID ...

TUT TUT! YOU MUSTN'T BELIEVE PREDICTIONS, OBELIX. REMEMBER THE HOROSCOPE*

* SEE THE MISSING SCROLL

YES BUT THIS TIME IT'S WRITTEN ON MY HAND! SHE DIDN'T PALM ME OFF WITH ANY OLD NONSENSE!

AND WHY CAN'T I BE AN AURIGA, ANYWAY? WHY DOES ASTERIX ALWAYS GET TO BE THE STAR?

OBELIX, MY FRIEND, YOU'RE IN MENHIRS!

OH REALLY? WELL, WHAT IF I WANT TO DROP THEM?

10

11

SENATOR BIFIDUS IS ON SITE ANSWERING QUESTIONS FROM SCRIBES WHO HAVE COME FROM EVERY DIRECTION TO COVER THE EVENT ...

A THRILLING MULTI-STAGE RACE FROM THE ALPS TO VESUVIUS, WITH A PRICELESS TROPHY FOR THE WINNER! LOOK, THESE CROWDS KNOW THEY'RE IN FOR A TREAT ...

JUST A MINUTE! **WHO'S FINANCING THIS?** THE ROMANS HAVE A RIGHT TO KNOW!

IT'S SIMPLE: WE HAVE A DEAL WITH LUPUS, THE BIG GARUM PRODUCER, THEY'RE SUPPLYING THE TROPHIES ...

IN RETURN, WE'VE ALLOWED THEM TO DISPLAY THEIR BANNERS AND HAND OUT AMPHORETTAS OF GARUM ALL ALONG THE ROUTE.

THE CONDIMENT **LVPVS** OF CHAMPIONS
THE ORIGINAL

GARUM!

THE CONDIMENT MADE FROM FERMENTED FISH GUTS, SO HIGHLY PRIZED BY THE ROMANS ...

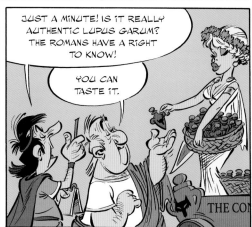

JUST A MINUTE! IS IT REALLY AUTHENTIC LUPUS GARUM? THE ROMANS HAVE A RIGHT TO KNOW!

YOU CAN TASTE IT.

THE CON

RAAAAH, IT REALLY IS, IT REALLY IS! AND IT REALLY IS GOOD!

THE FIRST-AID CHARIOT IS OVER THERE ...

I SAY, MADMAX, THIS HOT WATER IS DELICIOUS, IS IT NOT?

IT CERTAINLY IS, ECOTAX! THIS GARUM MAKES EVERYTHING TASTE QUITE EXQUISITE!

THAT'S THE BRETON CHARIOT!

AND THE LUSITANIAN CHARIOT'S OVER THERE!

HOW'S IT GOING, BITOVAMESS?

THE AXLE'S SEIZED, UNDADURESS, PASS ME THE GARUM!

12

IN THE NAME OF **JULIUS CAESAR** AND WITH GENEROUS SPONSORSHIP FROM **LUPUS** GARUM, I, BIFIDUS, PRONOUNCE ... UM ...

LVPVS THE CONDIMENT OF CHAMPIONS

"THE GREAT TRANSITALIC RACE OPEN."

... PRONOUNCE THE GREAT **TRANSITALIC RACE** OPEN!

CORONAVIRUS CORONAVIRUS CORONAVIRUS

LOOKS LIKE IT'S ALL ABOUT THAT ROMAN!

WELL, WHAT DO YOU EXPECT?

HE'S GOT A NICE SMILE.

IT'S A MASK, OBELIX!

THE WINNER WILL RECEIVE THE **TRANSITALIC CUP**, A SYMBOL OF OUR GLORIOUS, FAR-REACHING ROMAN ROADS ...

" ... OR ITS EQUIVALENT IN SESTER ... "

... OR ITS EQUIVALENT IN SESTERCES!!!

HEHE! WE'RE HERE FOR THE EQUIVALENT, MY BOY!

STAND BY FOR THE START ...

ONE OF THE KUSHITE COMPETITORS IS SMILING AT ME, ASTERIX! DO YOU THINK SHE LIKES ME?

NO! WHERE SHE'S FROM THEY'RE ALL IN DENIAL! CAREFUL, OBELIX, STAY FOCUSED!

♥ ♥ ♥

"WHEN I STRIKE THE GONG ..."

WHEN I STRIKE THE GONG ...

CORONAVIRUS CORONAVIRUS CORONAVIRUS

?!

THAT TREACHEROUS ROMAN'S STARTED! GO ON, OBELIX, GOOO!!

OK, HOLD ON TIGHT, DOGMATIX!

ARF!

The Gauls are leaving too! Let's go!

THE GOTH'S RIGHT, WOULD YOU BELIEVE! LET'S LEAVE!

YES, LET'S GO! BY JINN, GO!

THEY'VE STARTED! THEY'VE STARTED!

WHAT DO YOU MEAN STARTED? I HAVEN'T STRUCK THE GONG!

HURRY UP, BITOVAMESS. WE'RE GOING TO BE LATE ...

I'D BE SURPRISED, UNDADURESS. I HAVEN'T HEARD THE GONG.

15

18

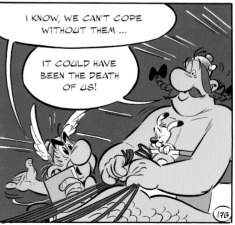

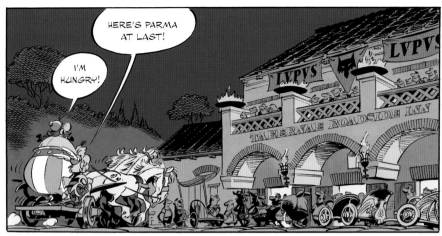

RIGHT. WHERE WERE WE? OH YES! THE HAM, OUR SPECIALITY. BEST EATEN IN VERY THIN SLI ...?!!

?!!

CHOMP CHOMP

EXSHELLENT! I'D LOVE ANOTHER SLICE.

SLURP

WHAT? SLICED HAM? THEY'LL BE HAVING POWDERED CHEESE NEXT!

A LITTLE WHILE LATER ...

I'M NOT SURE WHERE WE ARE: THERE AREN'T MANY ROMANS ...

PERFECTLY NORMAL, OBELIX. THERE'S MORE TO ITALY THAN ROMANS!

LIKE GAUL, ITALY HAS MANY DIFFERENT PEOPLES: VENETIANS, ETRUSCANS, UMBRIANS, OPICANS, MESSAPIANS, APULIANS ... AND CAESAR'S STRUGGLING TO CONTROL THEM.

GET SOME SLEEP. WE SET OFF WHEN THE COCK CROWS TOMORROW.

ONE ROMAN, TWO ROMANS, THREE ROMANS ...

LATE INTO THE NIGHT, THE LAST TEAMS ARE STILL ARRIVING.

COME ON, BITOVAMESS. WE'VE REACHED THE INN.

COMING, UNDADURESS! JUST CHECKING THE LEVELS ON THE HUBS!

I POINT.

AND AT THE CRACK OF DAWN ...

♪ A-COCCALA-DOODALA-DOO ♪

BUT, UNDADURESS, WE'VE ONLY JUST ARRIVED ...

GRRR WOOF

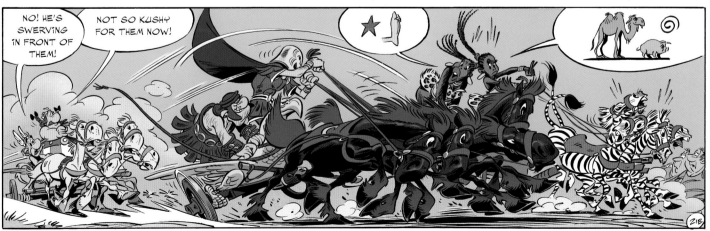

23

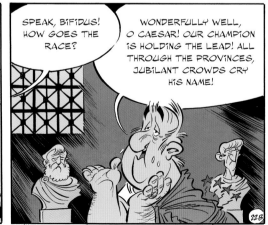

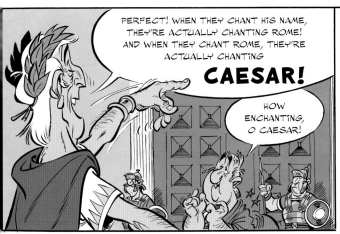

* FLORENCE

GETAFIX SAYS THAT PEOPLE EXPOSED TO SO MUCH BEAUTY CAN FEEL DIZZY AND COME OUT IN A COLD SWEAT!

REALLY? UM ... COULD YOU HOLD THE REINS A MOMENT?

SNIFF SNIFF

!?

CHOMP! CHOMP! WILD BOAR, REAL WHOLE WILD BOAR, **AT LAST!**

ROTISSERIE

SCROTCH!

SOME TIME LATER ...

GREAT! ALL THE OTHERS ARE WAY AHEAD OF US NOW!

EXACTLY WHAT YOU WERE SAYING, ASTERIX, DIZZY AND COLD SWEATS!

WE NEED TO FIND THE QUICKEST ROUTE TO SENA JULIA.

I CAN SEE SOMEONE OVER THERE.

24A

I DON'T THINK SHE UNDERSTANDS ...

MAYBE SHE DOESN'T SPEAK ITALIC?

BUT WHAT A LOVELY SMILE! AND IS IT JUST ME OR ARE HER EYES FOLLOWING US?

NOT NOW! STAY FOCUSED ON THE RACE!

LOOK! THEY'RE WAVING TO US ...

ARE YOU THE GAULISH CHARIOT? PLEASED TO MEET YOU! WE'RE NOT BIG FANS OF THE ROMAN CHAMPION HERE.

THIS WAY! WE'LL SHOW YOU A SHORT-CUT!

BUT FIRST YOU MUST TASTE OUR WINE! YOU'LL SEE, IT'S NOTHING LIKE YOUR BARLEY BEER!

POP

24B

26

SO FRIENDLY, THOSE ALCOH ... ITAL ... HIC! AND I CHIANTI STOP THINKING ABOUT THEIR WINE!

OH! LOOK, THERE'S A LEANING TOWER OVER THERE!

YOU'VE HAD TOO MUCH WINE, OBELIX!

ASTERIX, YOU'VE GONE BRIGHT RED!

YOU'RE THE ONE WHO'S RED! GIVE ME THE REINS AGAIN!

THESE ITALICS DO TEND TO LEAN, DON'T THEY ...

DON'T MAKE EXCUSES!

25A

CUTTING ACROSS ETRURIA'S ROLLING HILLS, OUR FRIENDS THE GAULS EVENTUALLY REJOIN THE ROMAN ROAD ...

LVPVS GARVM

THE CHAMPION'S CONDIMENT

BY THØR! THE TWØ GÅULS!

JUST ACT NATURAL, OBELIX.

??

25B

27

AND HERE ARE THE PASTAE, MY GAULISH FRIENDS! IT'S FROM THE EAST: THINLY SLICED DOUGH COOKED IN CREAM. EVEN IN ROME THEY DON'T MAKE IT THIS GOOD!

YOU SLICE EVERYTHING THINLY HERE!

... AND TO SEASON IT, AN AMPHORETTA OF GARUM FROM OUR SPONSOR, LUPUS.

?

WHAT EXACTLY IS THIS GARUM EVERYONE'S TALKING ABOUT?

ONLY THE **MOST FAMOUS** CONDIMENT! HAVEN'T YOU SEEN THE MOSAICS?

ON THE RIGHT BEFORE THE VESTIBULUM, PAST THE ATRIUM.

?

HERE, BACILLUS! THAT'S THE ADVANCE WE AGREED!

28A

THE SENATOR'S BANKING ON YOU TO ENSURE VICTORY FOR CORONAVIRUS.

?

THE BALANCE WILL BE PAID AT THE END OF THE RACE ... IF THE CHAMPION WINS, OF COURSE.

HE'LL WIN! I HOPE YOU REMEMBERED MY LITTLE CUT?

AND DON'T FORGET, WE ALSO SAID THE CHAMPION'S WEIGHT IN GARUM!

I'D PREFER MY OWN WEIGHT IN WILD BOAR IF THAT'S POSSIBLE ...

?

28B

* MARS IN THE SAMARTIAN LANGUAGE

32

HE'S A GUEST OF SENATOR BIFIDUS, WHO HAS A SMALL HOLIDAY VILLA NOT FAR FROM HERE!

MY FRIENDS, THIS GLORIOUS RACE HAS MADE ME PERSONA GRATA AT THE SENATE. THANKS TO YOU, I'M BACK TO RUNNING THE SESTERCES FOR THE ROMAN ROADS AS I SEE FIT!

AND DE FACTO TO FUNDING YOUR OWN LIFESTYLE!

LACTUS, THE ORGY'S READY!

JUST COMING, MOZZARELLA!

HEY, YOU TWO! YOU CAN'T PARK OUTSIDE THE SENATOR'S VILLA!

?!

BIFF

BAFF

LACTUS, DID YOU INVITE ANY GAULS TO THE ORGY?

BAFF

WAIT, I'LL BE BACK! WE WOULDN'T WANT THEM TO HAVE A WASTED JOURNEY.

BAFF

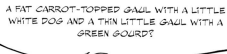

SOME TIME LATER, IN ROME ...

TWO GAULS, YOU SAY?

YES, O CAESAR, AND IF I COULD BORROW A FEW LEGIONARIES, TO HAVE THEM IMPRISONED ...

A FAT CARROT-TOPPED GAUL WITH A LITTLE WHITE DOG AND A THIN LITTLE GAUL WITH A GREEN GOURD?

EXACTLY! DO YOU KNOW THEM?

CAESAR SUDDENLY FEELS TIRED ...

SO WHAT ARE WE DOING ABOUT MY LEGIONARIES?

IMPRISON THE GAULS? SO THE WHOLE OF ITALY CAN SAY CAESAR'S AFRAID AND IS FIXING THE RACE?!

OH NO NO NO NO NO!!! GRACIOUS ME! FIXING'S NOT PRETTY AT ALL!

(36A)

DON'T PLAY THE INNOCENT! I KNOW WHAT YOUR CIMBRI ARE COOKING UP!

BUT, O GREAT CAESAR, IT WAS YOU YOURSELF WHO INSISTED THAT I ...

YOUR PLANS HAVE FAILED! AND YOU **DARE** TO ACCUSE CAESAR!

NNNO, NOT AT ALL, I ...

THANKS TO YOU, THIS RACE CONCEIVED TO ILLUSTRATE ROME'S BRILLIANCE WILL BE WON BY A [   ] BARBARIAN!

TO CYRENAICA!

I DON'T KNOW IT. WHAT'S IT LIKE?

ARID.

CAESAR NEEDS TO THINK. LEAVE HIM NOW, ACIDUS REFLUS.

SINE CURIS*

* NO WORRIES

36B

38

MEANWHILE, AT THE ROADSIDE INN IN TIBUR, THE REMAINING CONTESTANTS ARE CELEBRATING THE MASKED CHAMPION'S WITHDRAWAL ...

WELL DONE, YOU GAULS! WE SHOULD HAVE KNOWN CORONAVIRUS WAS JUST A JACKEY FOR ROMAN IMPERIALISM!

THESE ARE PINSAE FROM NEAPOLIS. DURUM WHEAT FLATBREADS TO GO WITH THE VARIOUS PASTAE.

SO ARE ZEBRAS FODDER-EFFICIENT?

SORRY TO BE A BORE ... YOU DON'T HAVE ANY BOAR DO YOU?

LEADER BOARD
LVPVS GARVM

CORONAVIRUS BACILLUS	XXX
NEFERSAYNEFER KVATLATIFER	XIX
OBELIX	XVIII
WOTALOADOV ADOV	XVI
ATTALOS	XVI
BITOVAM PADURESS	VII

CLINK

AURIGAE! LET'S CONTINUE THE RACE ON FAIR TERMS! MAY THE BEST TEAM WIN!

IF YOU ASK ME, THESE FLATBREADS WOULD BE BEST TEAMED WITH SOME TOPPING*!

CRICK CRACK

* A REMARKABLE PREMONITION FROM OBELIX, GIVEN THAT TOMATOES ARE NOT INTRODUCED INTO EUROPE FOR ANOTHER XVII CENTURIES.

AND AS THE COCK CROWS THE CONTESTANTS RACE CHEERFULLY ALONG THE APPIAN WAY, HEADING FOR CAMPANIA, SOUTH OF ROME ...

CLONK CLANK

THE INNKEEPER GAVE US SOME FLATBREADS FOR THE ROAD!

HMPH, NOTHING TO MAKE A MEAL OF!

PUTITTACROS FOR THE SPARTAN STANDARD: IS IT TRUE THAT THE RACE WAS FIXED?

VIVAJUVENTUS FROM THE LIGURIA BUGLE: ARE THEY SAYING A SENATOR'S INVOLVED?

Justatic of the Goth Herald: can you give us names?

LOOK! THEY'RE THE ONES WHO BROUGHT DOWN THE CHAMPION!

I KNOW THEM, THEY'RE GAULS! THE FAT ONE'S CALLED OBELIX!

OBELIX! OBELIX!

HE SMILED AT ME! HE SMILED AT ME!

SO, COMRADES, DAWDLING ARE WE?

38A

DAWDLING?

I'LL SHOW YOU DAWDLING! I'LL SHOW YOU DAWDLING!

?!!

?

?

BACK AT CRUISING SPEED, THE GAULS HAVE MANAGED TO SECURE A COMFORTABLE LEAD AND AFTER ABOUT A HUNDRED LEAGUES ...

THE BAY OF NEAPOLIS* AT LAST! AND BEYOND IT, MOUNT VESUVIUS AND THE FINISH LINE.

* NAPLES

38B

40

THE FINISH LINE! I'VE GOT 'EM!

?! CRONK

POTHOLE! POTHOLE!

OBELIX, MY FRIEND, YOU'RE ACTUALLY WINNING!

WELL? ISN'T THAT WHAT'S MEANT TO HAPPEN?

AAAAARGH!!! BIFIDUS! BIFIDUS!

THE GAULS! THE GAULS!

THEY WON!

THREE CHEERS FOR OBELIX, HIP HIP ...

HEY, LOOK AT CORONAVIRUS! HE'S TAKING OFF HIS MASK!

BUT ... IT'S NOT CORONAVIRUS!

IT'S ... IT'S ...

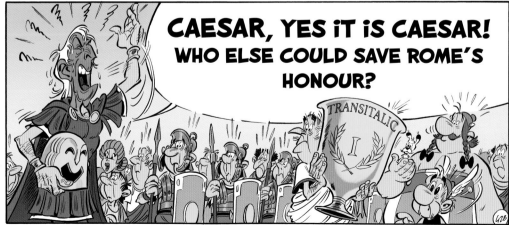

CAESAR, YES IT IS CAESAR! WHO ELSE COULD SAVE ROME'S HONOUR?

TRANSITALIC I

BUT HE HAS TO ADMIT HE RATHER ENJOYED THIS LITTLE RACE: ASPECTS OF IT REMINDED HIM OF HIS MISSPENT YOUTH ...

EVER THE SPORTSMAN, CAESAR RALLIES TO THE CRY OF HIS PEOPLE! IN THE NAME OF ROME AND ALL ITALY, CAESAR GIVES THE TRANSITALIC CUP TO THE GAULS!

LONG LIVE CAESAR!

HURRAY FOR OUR GREAT LEADER!

HERE'S TO ROME!

HERE'S TO ITALY!

UM ... I'VE BEEN THINKING, CHARIOT RACING'S NOT REALLY MY THING, HERE ONE DAY, THERE THE NEXT, NO PEACE, THE CONSTANT SPEED, GRABBING MEALS ON THE HOOF ...

AND ANYWAY, WITHOUT MY CO-AURIGA ... NO, I'D NEVER HAVE WON. HERE, ASTERIX, THIS IS FOR YOU!

THANK YOU, MY KIND FRIEND OBELIX, IT WAS A GREAT RACE!

43A

WE ALL EARNED THIS CUP, I'D LIKE TO HAND IT ON TO OUR KUSHITE FRIENDS!

NO REASON WE SHOULDN'T SHARE TOO, BY MARX!

DELICIOUS DOWN TO THE LAST DROP *LVPVS GARVM*

I DISAGREE! THE CUP SHOULD GO TO THE MOST PERSISTENT TEAM: **THE LUSITANIANS**, BY ZEUS!

TAKE THE EQUIVALENT IN SESTERCES, UNDADURESS! WE'RE GOING TO NEED A NEW CHARIOT!

BLONK TUNK

FERRI + CONRAD

THE END

With heartfelt thanks to Anthea Bell for her wonderful translation work on ASTERIX over the years.
Les Éditions Albert René and Orion Children's Books

Asterix titles available now

ORION CHILDREN'S BOOKS

First published in Great Britain in 2017 by Hodder & Stoughton

1 3 5 7 9 10 8 6 4 2

ASTERIX®-OBELIX®-DOGMATIX®
Original edition © 2017 Les Éditions Albert René
English translation © 2017 Les Éditions Albert René
Original title: *Astérix et la Transitalique*
Exclusive licensee: Hachette Children's Group
Translator: Adriana Hunter
Typography: Arvind Shah

The right of Jean-Yves Ferri to be identified as the author of this work and
the right of Didier Conrad to be identified as the illustrator of this work have been
asserted by them in accordance with the Copyright, Designs and Patents Act 1988.

All rights reserved.

A CIP catalogue record for this book is available from the British Library.

ISBN 978-1-5101-0401-3 (cased)
ISBN 978-1-5101-0403-7 (Indian paperback)
ISBN 978-1-5101-0402-0 (ebook)

Printed and bound in Italy by Printer Trento S.R.L
The paper and board used in this book are from well-managed forests and other responsible sources.

Orion Children's Books
An imprint of Hachette Children's Group
Part of Hodder & Stoughton
Carmelite House, 50 Victoria Embankment
London EC4Y 0DZ
An Hachette UK Company

www.hachette.co.uk
www.asterix.com
www.hachettechildrens.co.uk

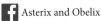 Asterix and Obelix

Asterix ®

Have you read them all?

    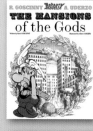 

www.asterix.com   ASTERIX®-OBELIX®-DOGMATIX® / © 2017 LES ÉDITIONS ALBERT RENÉ/GOSCINNY - UDERZO

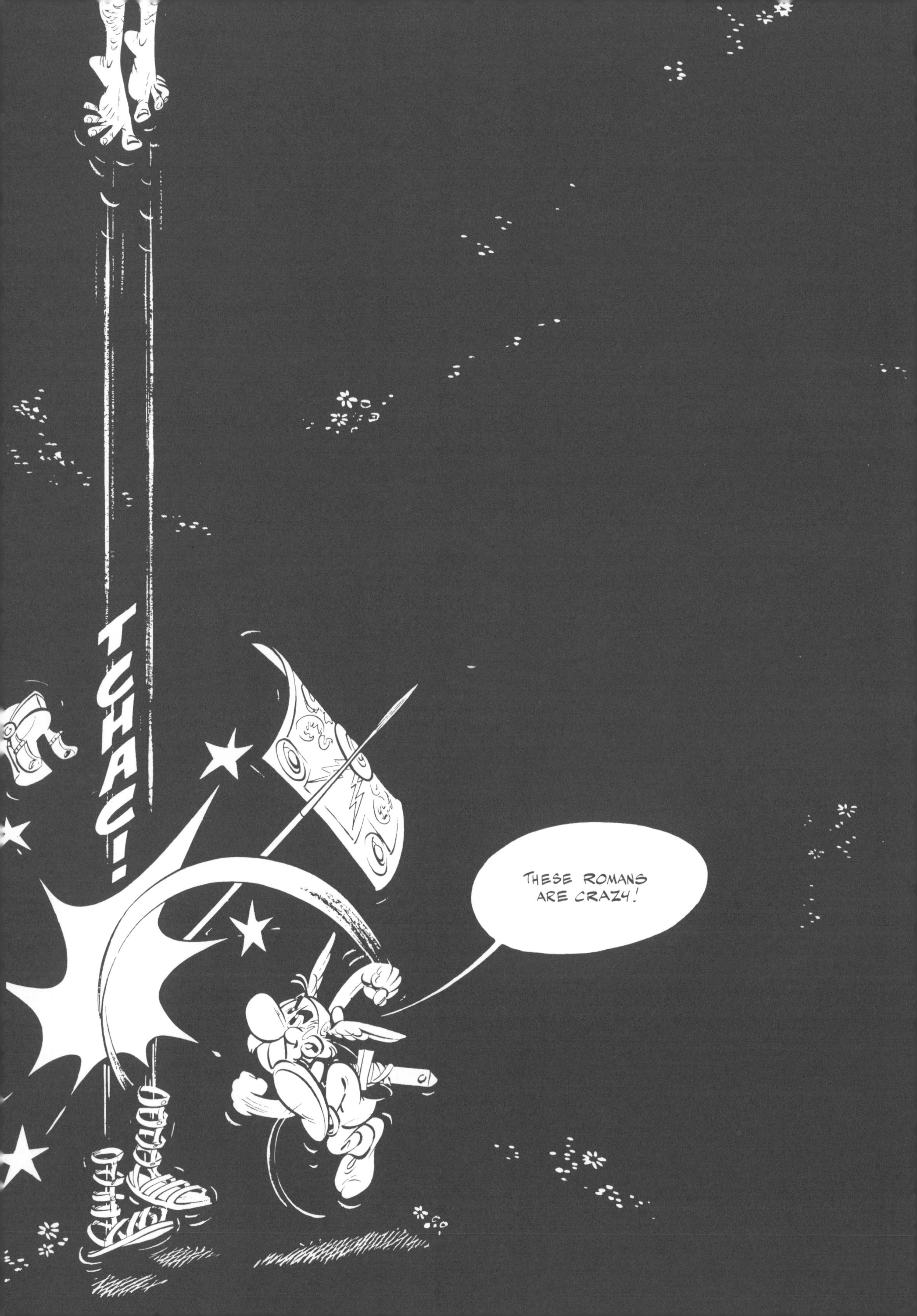
TCHAC!
THESE ROMANS ARE CRAZY!